iVy + BEAN

BOOK 10

More Praise for IVY + BEAN!

★ "Just right for kids moving on from beginning readers . . .
illustrations deftly capture the girls' personalities and the tale's
humor. . . . Barrows' narrative brims with sprightly dialogue."
—*Publishers Weekly*, starred review

★ "In the tradition of Betsy and Tacy, Ginnie and Genevra, come
two new friends, Ivy and Bean. . . . The deliciousness is in the
details here. . . . Will make readers giggle."
—*Booklist*, starred review

★ "Ivy and Bean are irresistible."
—*Kirkus Reviews*, starred review

"A charming new series." —*People*

"Ivy and Bean are a terrific buddy combo." —*Chicago Tribune*

"This is a great chapter book for students who have recently
crossed the independent reader bridge."
—*School Library Journal*

"Annie Barrows' simple and sassy text will draw in both the
reluctant reader and the young bookworm. Fans of Beverly
Cleary's Beezus and Ramona will enjoy this cleverly written and
illustrated tale of sibling rivalry and unexpected friendship."
—*BookPage*

iVy + BEAN
TAKE THE CASE

BOOK 10

written by annie barrows + illustrated by sophie blackall

chronicle books · san francisco

To Victoria Rock, mentor, strategist,
and fellow subversive, with gratitude.

—A. B. + S. B.

This is a component of a boxed set. Not for individual retail.

ISBN 978-1-4521-4228-9

The Library of Congress has cataloged the original edition as follows:

Library of Congress Cataloging-in-Publication Data
Barrows, Annie.
Ivy + Bean take the case / written by Annie Barrows ; illustrated by Sophie Blackall.
p. cm. — (Ivy + Bean ; bk. 10)
Summary: After watching a movie about a detective on the television,
Bean decides to set up shop as a private investigator—and she and Ivy start
looking for mysteries to solve.
ISBN 978-1-4521-0699-1 (alk. paper)
1. Bean (Fictitious character : Barrows)—Juvenile fiction. 2. Ivy (Fictitious character:
Barrows)—Juvenile fiction. 3. Private investigators—Juvenile fiction. 4. Best friends—
Juvenile fiction. 5. Humorous stories. [1. Mystery and detective stories. 2. Private
investigators—Fiction. 3. Best friends—Fiction. 4. Friendship—Fiction. 5. Humorous
stories.] I. Blackall, Sophie. ill. II. Title. III. Title: Ivy and Bean take the case. IV. Series:
Barrows, Annie. Ivy + Bean ; bk. 10.

PZ7.B27576Iys 2013
813.6—dc23

2012046876

Manufactured in China.

MIX
Paper from
responsible sources
FSC™ C020056

Book design by Sara Gillingham Studio.
Typeset in Blockhead and Candida.
The illustrations in this book were rendered in Chinese ink.

2 3 4 5 LEO 17 16 15 14 13

Chronicle Books LLC
680 Second Street, San Francisco, California 94107

Chronicle Books—we see things differently.
Become part of our community at www.chroniclekids.com.

CONTENTS

BLACK AND WHITE AND TOUGH ALL OVER

Bean wasn't allowed to watch television. Or music videos. Bean's mom said she could watch two movies a week, but they had to be movies where everyone was good. There couldn't be any bad words. There couldn't be any mean people. There couldn't be anyone smoking a cigarette or wearing tiny clothes. There were only about ten movies that followed all these rules. Luckily, Bean liked all ten of them. She watched them over and over.

Bean's mom said ten movies were plenty. She said kids Bean's age should be using their imaginations instead of watching TV. She said fresh air was more important than movies.

And then what did she do?

She made Bean watch a movie. It was her favorite movie, she said. Everyone should see it at least once, she said. The movie was called *Seven Falls*, but it wasn't about waterfalls or even the leaf-falling kind of fall, which is what Bean had guessed. It was about a guy named Al Seven. Boy, was he tough! He was so tough he talked without moving his lips, and some of it was bad words.

He was also kind of mean. Everyone in the movie was kind of mean, plus they all smoked cigarettes. They didn't wear tiny clothes, but that was the only rule they didn't break.

"I can't believe you're letting me watch this," said Bean.

"*Seven Falls* is a classic," said Bean's mom. "It's one of the greatest movies ever made."

"Don't be a stooge," said Al Seven to another movie guy. That was pretty mean, but Bean pretended not to notice, because this was one of the greatest movies ever made. Al Seven was also in black and white, but Bean knew she was supposed to imagine he was in color. "What is it about dames?" asked Al Seven, walking slowly down a rainy street. "They break your heart, I guess," he answered himself.

That was the end.

Bean's mom let out a big, happy sigh. "Wasn't that amazing? Did you get it?"

Get what? Bean wasn't sure, but she nodded. "I'm going to be just like Al Seven when I grow up."

Her mother raised one eyebrow. "You'd better not be."

But then again, why wait, thought Bean. She could start being like Al Seven now. She slumped over and put her feet on the coffee table. "Whaddaya say we watch it again, pal?" she said.

Her mom raised both eyebrows. "What I say is don't call me pal and take your feet off the table."

That hadn't worked. Bean took her feet off the table. "Dames," she said sadly. "They break your heart."

Her mom's eyebrows were almost inside her hair. "Oh dear," she said.

+ + + + +

It took Bean a long time to go to sleep that night. She couldn't stop thinking about Al Seven and his black-and-white world. It didn't seem like the real world, the world on Pancake Court that Bean lived in. People in Al Seven's

world were tough, and they didn't laugh very much. They didn't do normal stuff like go to school and the grocery store. They walked down alleys and wore hats. But the most un-normal thing about Al Seven's world was the mysteries. There were mysteries all over the place.

Bean untwisted her pajamas and thought about that. A mystery was a question you couldn't find the answer to. In Al Seven's world, the mysteries were things like Who took Hester's jewels? or Where was Sammy La Barba on the night of May twelfth? Bean didn't have any jewels and she sure as heck didn't know anyone named Sammy La Barba, but there were plenty of questions that she didn't have answers to. Millions of them. For instance, Who thought of money? Not even grown-ups knew the answer to that question. But Bean had other questions, too, like What's inside the cement thing in the front yard? What's behind the Tengs' fence and why do they lock it up? and What's the matter with the mailman? When she asked these questions, her parents usually said something like It's none of your business. That meant that there was an answer, but they didn't want her to know it.

Bean smiled toughly at her dark ceiling. They didn't want her to know things. Just like Sammy La Barba didn't want Al Seven to know where he was on the night of May twelfth. But Al Seven had figured it out, because he was a private investigator. Private investigators got to the bottom of mysteries. They solved them. They snuck around. They spied. They asked the hard questions. They sat in their cars and rubbed their faces until they came up with the answers. Then they walked down alleys in the rain.

That's what Bean was going to do. First thing tomorrow morning. "None of your business!" she muttered. "Ha!"

PIRVATE INSTEVIGATOR

Al Seven had a cool office with his name on the door. Bean could do that, easy-peasy. She began with the desk. Bean had a good board, and she had two triangle things that were called sawhorses even though they didn't look anything like horses. She put the sawhorses on the front lawn, and then she put the board on top of the sawhorses. Desk! The spinny chair was a little harder. Bean had to yank it up the basement stairs, yank, yank, yank. And just when she got to the top, it fell back down most of the stairs. It was already broken, but it was more broken after it fell down the stairs.

"What the heck are you doing, Bean?" called her father from the kitchen.

"I'm trying to get this chair up the stairs!" shouted Bean.

"Do you want help?"

Bean thought about that. Al Seven had a helper, a lady named Dolly. Mostly, Dolly lit Al's cigarette, but Bean figured she would have carried a chair if Al had asked her to. "Yes, please."

Her dad came down to the basement and carried the spinny chair up the stairs. He even carried it out to the front yard.

"Thanks, pal," said Bean.

Her dad said, "Don't call me pal. You're welcome."

Bean put the chair behind the desk and sat in it. She spun around. Pretty good. But she wasn't done yet. She needed to look tough enough to solve a mystery. She needed a hat. She was pretty sure there was one upstairs, in the closet of things no one wanted.

She was right! On the highest shelf of things no one wanted, covered with dust, was a hat. It was sort of grayish, sort of brownish. It smelled funny. When Bean put it on, she could hardly see. It was a little dangerous, walking around in that hat, but Al Seven said, "Danger makes me laugh."

While Bean was climbing down from the shelf, she found something she hadn't expected, something great. It was a telephone, an old one with two parts and a cord. Perfect! Al Seven was always slamming the phone down on people. Bean slammed the phone

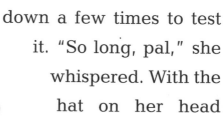

down a few times to test it. "So long, pal," she whispered. With the hat on her head and the phone under her arm, Bean went downstairs to her mom's recycling bin.

Bean's mom's recycling bin was always full of important-looking papers. Papers with rubber stampings all over them. Papers with typing in three different colors. Papers with sticky notes. Today was a good day in the bin. Papers were spilling out the sides. Also big envelopes. And file folders! What a haul! Since she was already down on the floor, Bean took a look in her mom's wastebasket. Five thousand lipstick tissues and a plastic picture of an alligator lying on a log. Words coming out of the alligator's mouth said, "Sure I'm working. I'm working so fast you can't see it."

Bean stared at the plastic picture for a long time. Was the alligator working or was it supposed to be funny? Did grown-ups think it was funny? If they did, why? It was a mystery.

But, Bean decided, not a very interesting one.
With her hat, her phone, and an armful of
paper, Bean went outside.

+ + + + +

Bean was a good artist. She
could draw nice stuff like
flowers and cute bugs and
dancing bagels, but she
could also draw serious
stuff like science pictures
and pyramids. Her sign was
serious. She wanted it to
look like a real, grown-up
sign. Al Seven's sign said Al
Seven, Private Investigator.
Bean wanted a sign like
that. She began to write in
big, serious letters.

Bean's last name was really long. It was so long that sometimes she mixed up the letters.

She mixed up the letters.

Bean got another piece of paper. Bean, she wrote in big, serious letters. Good.

Private. Good.

Investigator. Oops. Instevigator.

Bean got another piece of paper.

Bean. Good.

Pirvate. Oops.

Bean got another piece of paper.

Bean. Good.

Prva—oops. Bean crumpled the paper and threw it on the ground.

She got another piece of paper.

Bean. Good.

P. Good.

I. Good.

Done. Whew.

Bean taped her sign to the plum tree. She put her hat on her head. She put the papers and file folders on the desk. She made her eyes into slits and looked around Pancake Court. She watched Jake the Teenager walk out of his house with a gigantic shopping bag. "So long, pal," she muttered. She picked up the phone and slammed it down. She was tough. She was ready. She was ready for her first mystery.

UNDER COVER JOB

In front of every house on Pancake Court, there was a yard. Then there was a sidewalk. After that came the curb, and then came the street. At the front of every yard, near the sidewalk, there was a little cement rectangle. Every house on Pancake Court had one of these little cement rectangles in front of it, and every little cement rectangle had a small hole in it. Bean had known this for years.

But what was under the rectangle? Bean didn't know. It could be a tunnel that led to the center of the Earth. It could be anything!

Bean crouched over the little cement rectangle in front of her house and peered into the hole. No good. She couldn't see anything. She lay down on the grass and put her eye over the hole. Nothing but darkness.

"What's down there?" said a voice.

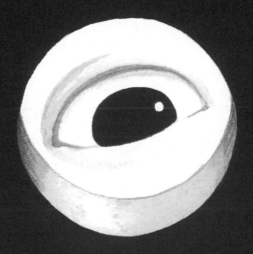

"Yikes!" squawked Bean, flopping over like a pancake.

It was Ivy, leaning over her. "What're you doing?"

It's hard to be tough while you're lying flat on your back, but Bean tried. "I'm cracking a case."

"You're what?" asked Ivy.

"It means solving a mystery," Bean said. She sat up. "I'm practicing to be a private investigator. P. I. for short."

"Pi?" Ivy said. "3.1415—"

"No, not that one. P. I. stands for private investigator. You know, someone who solves mysteries. Like Al Seven."

"Al who?" asked Ivy.

So Bean explained everything about Al Seven and *Seven Falls.* For a while, Ivy thought Al Seven *was* seven, but soon she understood.

Bean told her about how Al Seven found clues and rubbed his face. She told Ivy about how Al Seven snuck after people and spied on them and asked them the hard questions. How Al Seven spied on Sammy La Barba and saw him put money in a mailbox. And then about how Al Seven gave all the money to a girl named Lola.

"Why'd he do that?" asked Ivy.

Bean shrugged. "Don't know. But then he sits in his car for a long time and then the police come and some newspaper guys, and he's a big hero. But he doesn't care, and he walks off alone in an alley."

"Wow." Ivy was impressed.

"So," Bean said. "I'm going to be a P. I. and I'm going to solve mysteries."

Ivy looked around Bean's front yard. "What mystery are you solving now?"

"The Mystery of What's Under the Cement Rectangle," Bean answered.

"Hey!" Ivy said. "I've always wondered about that!"

"That's what makes it a mystery," said Bean. She rolled over and looked into the hole again. "I was trying to see into it, but it was too dark, so now—" She hooked her finger into the hole. "Ew. It's slimy." But Al Seven wouldn't let a little slime stop him, and neither would Bean. She pulled. The cement rectangle made a scraping sound. Just as she thought: It was a lid. She pulled harder. More scraping. She pulled really hard. The cement rectangle popped upward.

"Wow," said Ivy, bending over the rectangle in the grass.

Underneath the cement lid, down below the grass, there was a rectangular space full of slime. In the middle of the space stood a gray machine with a dial on it. Pipes came from its sides and disappeared into the ground.

"Hey, look at that!" It was Sophie S. from down the street, bending over Bean. "I always wanted to know what was under there."

"The Mystery of What's Under the Cement Rectangle has now been solved," Bean said. It felt good to have an answer.

Sophie S. peered down into the hole. "You think the same thing is inside all of them?"

"There's only one way to find out," said Bean the P. I.

SPECIAL DELIVERY

All around Pancake Court, rectangular cement lids lay beside slimy cement holes.

"I don't think it counts as a mystery," said Prairie. She was nine. She argued a lot.

"Sure it does," said Bean. "It was the Mystery of What's Under the Cement Rectangle. I solved it."

"I feel a lot better now that I know for sure there aren't monsters in there," said Sophie S.

"It's not mysterious," argued Prairie. "It's just pipes in the dirt."

The nerve! Bean made her eyes into slits. "Look, I'm almost a private investigator, so I know about what's a mystery and what's not."

Prairie made a snorty sound. "Hey, Dino!" she called as he zipped by on his skateboard. "Guess what Bean and Ivy are doing?!"

He skidded into the grass. "What?"

"We're solving mysteries," said Bean firmly.

Dino looked around. "What mysteries?"

Bean looked at Prairie. "The Mystery of the Sleeping Mailman."

+ + + + + +

"Shh!" whispered Ivy.

They tiptoed down Ivy's driveway and stuffed themselves behind a bush. Very carefully, they leaned out and looked toward the mail truck parked at the curb. Inside, the mailman was lying across the two front seats. His eyes were closed. His mouth was open. He had earphones in his ears.

"I don't see what's so mysterious about him," said Prairie. "He's just sleeping."

"He does it every day," whispered Bean. "He whizzes around Pancake Court, parks in front of Ivy's house, and falls asleep for two hours. Why does he sleep in the middle of the day? It's a mystery."

Prairie looked doubtful, but Bean didn't wait for her to argue. She moved silently to a tree near the mail truck and beckoned for Ivy to follow her. One by one, Ivy and Sophie S. and Dino and Prairie came to her side. Together, they watched the mailman breathe in and out.

Bean remembered how Al Seven had given a big sigh and walked toward Sammy La Barba. Bean pulled down her hat, gave a big sigh, and walked toward the mail truck.

Silently, she stood at the open door of the truck.

The mailman breathed in and out.

Silently, the other kids gathered around her.

The mailman breathed in and out.

Silently, Bean bent down to look at the mailman. What was the matter with him?

The mailman breathed in and out.

Silently, the other kids bent down to look at the mailman. What was the matter with him?

The mailman's eyes clicked open. He screamed.

+ + + + + +

"But now we know," Bean was saying. "We didn't know before, and now we do."

"He's just tired because his baby cries all night!" said Prairie.

"It's not very mysterious," agreed Dino. Ruby and Trevor, who lived down the street, nodded. They'd come outside when the mailman screamed, but they didn't think a sleepy mailman was mysterious either.

Ivy's cheeks got pink. "Look! No one knew why he slept in his truck. Now we know. The mystery was solved by Bean, P. I."

Prairie shook her head.

"Fine," said Bean. "I'll solve my next mystery alone. With Ivy."

"What's the mystery?" asked Sophie S.

"I can't tell you, but it's a good one," said Bean, crossing her arms.

"A really good one," added Ivy. "Very mysterious and strange."

"Strange?" said Sophie S. "Really?"

Bean frowned. It wasn't exactly strange.

"Yeah!" said Ivy. "So strange it would make your hair stand on end."

Trevor made an I-don't-believe-you noise. "What is it?"

"So mysterious that your skin would crawl," Ivy went on. Bean looked at her, worried. Their skin probably wouldn't crawl, exactly. "So incredible—"

"WHAT?" yelled Trevor, Ruby, and Prairie at the same time.

"The Tengs!" Bean shouted. "What do they keep locked behind their fence?"

There was a silence. "I've always wondered that," said Trevor.

+ + + + + +

It was a beautiful garden. There were flowers everywhere, roses and big blue things that Bean didn't know the name of. There was a cherry tree with shiny red cherries on it. There was a stone lion and a table and a white bench where the Tengs' cat snoozed in the sun.

There were even artichokes with purple tops growing on stems. Bean had never known that artichokes grew on stems. It was pretty. It was nice.

But it was not mysterious.

Or strange.

Or incredible or skin-crawling.

Bean climbed down the chair on top of the other chair on top of the table. Slowly, she turned to face Ivy, Sophie S., Dino, Prairie, Ruby, and Trevor.

WHAT'S UP?

Things were not going the way Bean wanted.

Dino pulled a blade of grass from the lawn. "Look!" he yelled. "It's the Mystery of the Piece of Grass!"

Sophie S. kicked off her flip-flop. "Oh my gosh! It's the Mystery of the Missing Shoe!"

Prairie held her finger in front of her face. "I see a mysterious hand!"

Bean felt herself get hot and embarrassed. No one laughed at Al Seven. She was doing exactly what he did. Why was he cool and tough, while Bean was hot and embarrassed? It wasn't fair.

Ivy stomped her foot. "There *are* strange and mysterious things on Pancake Court. You just don't notice them."

Sophie S. and Ruby giggled. Trevor said, "You're loonies. Nothing strange ever happens around here. This is the most boring place in the world." Trevor and Ruby went to school at home. They got bored a lot. "I'll bet you fifty cents you can't show me one strange thing on Pancake Court. One!"

Bean looked quickly around Pancake Court for one strange thing. Houses. Yards. Cars. Mr. Columbi going to work. Two cats. A bicycle. Jake the Teenager and his shopping bag. Nothing strange. She had to think. She could say she had a buried treasure map, and then she could draw it really quick.

Trevor made a snorty sound. "It's the case of the missing mystery!" he said. Then he laughed.

"Bean's hat is pretty strange," giggled Prairie.

Bean yanked her hat off. "Come on, Ivy," she said, as toughly as she could. "We have mysteries to solve." Ivy nodded in an Al Sevenish way. "Look tough," muttered Bean. Ivy rubbed her face, and they walked quickly away around Pancake Court.

Bean needed a mystery on the double. A lost puppy. Or a lost necklace. Or strange people hiding behind trees. Or smudged handprints on cars. Or anything. "Do you see anything that looks mysterious?" she whispered to Ivy.

"Mrs. Trantz's rocks?" suggested Ivy. Mrs. Trantz had white rocks in her front yard instead of grass. Why would anyone do that?

"Not good enough," said Bean. "We need something strange and mysterious, like—" She stopped. "That," she said, pointing.

It was Dino's house she was pointing at, but the house wasn't the mysterious part. The mysterious part was a bright yellow rope that dangled from the roof of the house to the ground. One end was tied around the chimney. The other end was sitting in the middle of Dino's front lawn.

"What is that?" asked Ivy.

"It's a mystery!" said Bean. Whew! Just in the nick of time!

Ivy began to smile. "It's a rope of mystery."

"Still not scared!" hollered Trevor. He and Dino were picking bark off sticks and throwing it at each other.

"Hey, Dino!" called Bean. "What's that rope on your house?"

Dino stopped throwing bark and looked at his house. He frowned. "I don't know." He threw another piece of bark. Then he came to stand next to Bean and Ivy. "It wasn't there before."

"So this is the first time you've seen it?" asked Bean.

Dino nodded. Then he frowned some more. "Weird."

"Strange," Bean corrected him.

"And mysterious," said Ivy.

Trevor threw a piece of bark at Dino. It bounced off. "What are you guys doing?" he asked, coming closer.

"I'm going to ask my mom," said Dino. "She probably did it. Or something."

Bean and Ivy and Trevor watched the rope until Dino and his mom came back. Dino's mom looked busy. She had two pairs of glasses on her head and a sticky note on her shirt that said Don't forget Friday!

"That," said Dino, pointing at the rope.

Dino's mom looked up to the chimney. She looked down to the grass. She frowned. She went to the rope and pulled it gently. She frowned more. "That's weird," she said. Still frowning, she turned to Dino. "If you went up on that roof, there's going to be trouble, young man!"

"I didn't do it!" yelped Dino. "If I did it, I wouldn't ask you about it!"

"Right. Sorry." His mom shook her head. "I have no idea what it is. I didn't put it there. I couldn't, actually. We don't have a ladder that goes all the way up to the roof." She frowned again. "Strange."

Bean looked at Trevor and wiggled her eyebrows, which was sort of like sticking out your tongue, but you couldn't get in trouble for it.

Dino's mom stared at the rope for a little while longer and then shrugged. "I don't know.

But I have to finish this e-mail. We'll figure it out later." She went back in the house.

Bean waited patiently until she was gone. Then she turned around to Dino and Trevor. "Well, whaddaya know?" she said. She put her hat on again. "We've got a mystery on Pancake Court!"

PANCAKE FALLS

The first thing Bean did was dust for fingerprints. Al Seven was always dusting for fingerprints. Here's how you dust for fingerprints: First, you sprinkle powder. Then you gently dust it away. And then you whip out your magnifying glass and peer through it, and—ta-DA!—you see the fingerprints of the bad guy!

Bean didn't really understand how that part worked, but the dusting part was fun.

Gently, Bean sprinkled baby powder on the yellow rope. Gently, she brushed it away with a paintbrush.

Everyone leaned in to look.

Bean whipped out her magnifying glass and peered through it. She saw rope. "Just as I thought," she said. She nodded slowly and made her voice low. "There are no fingerprints here."

Ivy nodded slowly, too. "No fingerprints."

"But that doesn't help us at all!" said Dino. "Why is there a rope on my house?"

Bean made her eyes very narrow. "Time will tell." She put her magnifying glass in her pocket and looked at the sky. Speaking of time, it was almost time for dinner.

Her dad came out on the front porch. "Bean!" he called.

"You can't leave now!" said Dino.

Al Seven never said good-bye. He said things like "Catch you later, chump." But that was really mean, so Bean said, "Bye, you guys. See you tomorrow."

The next morning was completely regular—
yawn, splash, stumble, cereal, banana, where's
my jacket, somebody took it, oh here it is,
bye—until Bean got outside and saw Ivy. Ivy
was standing on the sidewalk in front of her
house, watching the
ground. She was watching
the ground so seriously that
she didn't hear Bean running
up behind her.

"Bug?" asked Bean. She hoped it was a big one.

Ivy shook her head and pointed.

The yellow rope had grown in the night. Where it had ended the day before, on Dino's lawn, there was now a knot. More yellow rope went across the lawn, circled around Dino's tree, down his driveway, and next door to Ivy's house, where it snaked in and out of her fence posts and ended at her stairs.

"Wow," said Bean. It was a real, genuine mystery.

"Yeah," said Ivy. She turned around and looked at Bean carefully. "Did you do it?"

"Me?" squawked Bean. "No! No way!" She stopped squawking and looked carefully at Ivy. "It wasn't you, was it?"

Ivy shook her head. "No. I thought it was you."

"How would I get up to Dino's chimney?" Bean pointed out.

They both turned and stared at the rope. "It's the real thing," muttered Ivy. Bean nodded.

They both tried to look tough. But they couldn't. "Cool!" they yelled at the same time.

+ + + + + +

For some reason, Dino didn't think it was cool. "It's creepy," he said, when they met up that afternoon. Sophie S. and Ruby and Trevor nodded. They thought it was creepy, too.

"Why?" asked Bean. She looked at the yellow rope winding in and out of Ivy's fence. "It's just a rope."

"But somebody put it there," said Dino. "And we don't know why."

Bean nodded. "Yeah. Pretty strange, isn't it?"

"A real mystery," said Ivy.

This time, nobody argued, not even Prairie. Ha. "So you want to find out who did it?" asked Bean.

"Yeah," said Dino.

"Yeah," said Ruby and Trevor and Sophie S. Prairie nodded.

"Okay," said Bean. "I'll take the case." She tried to remember what Al Seven said when he took the case. She pulled her hat down and said, "Watch out, Mr. Whoever-tied-the-yellow-rope. You've met your match."

HOUSE CALLS

Ivy came down her stairs holding a gigantic pair of scissors. "My mom says not to cut anything thick with them." She handed them to Bean.

"I've seen ropes that are way thicker than this," said Bean. She knelt by the end of the rope and started cutting. "Okay," she said, when she had finally done it. "This is our sample. Let's get to work." She stood up.

"Where are you going?" asked Dino.

"We're going to find our suspect," said Bean.

"Our what?" asked Prairie.

"Suspects are people who might have done it," explained Bean. "We're going to look in people's basements and sheds and stuff. If we see a yellow rope, then we know that person is probably the one who's doing it. Get it?"

They got it.

"First stop is your house," said Bean to Dino.

"My house?!" shouted Dino. "I didn't do anything!"

"Okay. But what about your dad?" asked Bean. "Or Crum . . . I mean, Matt?" Everyone called Dino's brother Crummy Matt except Dino. It was hard to remember to call him just plain Matt when Dino was around.

"It wasn't my dad or Matt," said Dino. "They're on a field trip. But you can look in our basement if you want."

Dino's basement was surprising, but not because there was yellow rope in it. There were lots of paintings in it and they were all of clouds. Dino's dad had painted them.

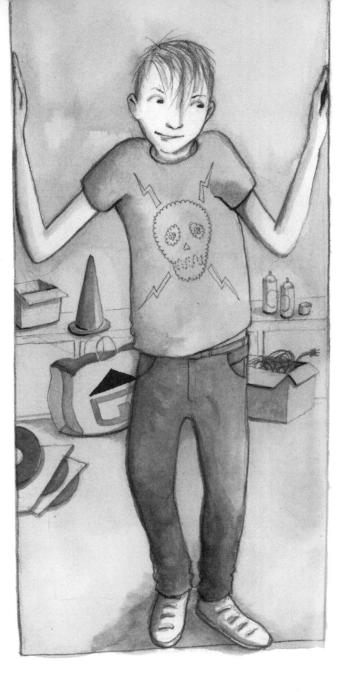

At Sophie S.'s house, they kept their junk in the garage. There was plenty of junk in there. But no rope.

Ruby and Trevor's house was the neatest place in the world. Even in the shed, all the stuff was in baskets and each basket had a little sign on it. Ivy and Bean found green garden string, but no rope.

They went to Prairie's house, Sophie W.'s house, and Jake the Teenager's house. Jake the Teenager said his gecko was sleeping, so they couldn't come in. But he said he knew for sure he didn't have any yellow rope. Then they went to Ivy's house and Bean's house, too, just to be fair. They saw many interesting things. But not one of the things they saw was a yellow rope.

After that, everyone went to Bean's office to rest. Bean sat in her spinny chair, thinking. They had done all the kid-houses. Eight kid-houses, no rope. That left seven—no, eight—houses with no kids or tiny kids or grown-up kids. How was she going to get into those basements and sheds? Could she sneak in? She might have to break a window. Al Seven would do it in a second. Al Seven had probably never been grounded.

Ivy cleared her throat.

Bean spun.

Ivy cleared her throat again.

Bean looked at her. What?

Ivy wiggled her eyebrows. She tossed her hair.

Bean gave Ivy a bug-eyed look. *What?*

Ivy tapped her nose.

"What?!" Bean shouted.

I HAV AN IDEA

"I have an idea!" yelled Ivy. Everyone looked up. "Well, I do," she said. "I read a book that said you can tell when people are lying if they look to one side or cover their mouths or pull their ears while they're talking."

"Pull their ears? Who pulls their ears?" asked Sophie S., confused.

Bean pulled her ear. "It doesn't make me feel like lying."

"No," said Ivy. "It doesn't make you lie to pull your ear, but if you *are* lying, you'll pull it."

"Oh." Bean thought about that. "Great."

"Don't you get it?" asked Ivy. "We go around Pancake Court. We ring the doorbell and show people the rope. We say, 'Have you seen this rope before?' Everyone will say no, but if they look to one side or cover their mouths or pull their ears while they say it, they're lying! And then," Ivy smiled, "we have our suspect!"

PLAN AHEAD!

The Tengs weren't home.

+ + + + + +

Mr. Columbi scratched his neck. "Nope."

+ + + + + +

Kalia said, "Potty, potty, potty!"

Kalia's mom said, "Sorry, I don't think so, girls. Oh, honey, yuck!"

+ + + + + +

Mr. Ensor, who was really incredibly old, rubbed his forehead and said, "Don't need any rope. Thanks anyway."

"I love your hat!" squealed Eleanor-who-lived-in-the-blue-house. "A rope? Give them enough rope! Ahahahahaha! You kids are wild! Great!"

+ + + + + +

Mr. Larson was talking on his phone. "Not now. No. Rope? No. I'm not talking to you, Frank. It's these kids. No, no rope! Come back later or something."

Mrs. Larson said, "Get off the phone, Bennett! It's not ours, Bean, sorry."

+ + + + + +

Fester the dog barked. There was nobody at his house except him.

+ + + + + +

Ivy took a deep breath. She took one step onto Mrs. Trantz's front path. Like magic, the door opened, and Mrs. Trantz was standing on her porch.

"What are you doing in my garden, little girl?" yelled Mrs. Trantz.

"Hi, Mrs. Trantz," began Ivy politely.

"Don't Mrs. Trantz me!" yelled Mrs. Trantz, not politely. "What are those children doing on the sidewalk there? Is that Bernice?" She peered at Bean, who was bravely standing at the edge of Mrs. Trantz's white gravel, and at the other kids, who were sort of crouched in the hedge next door. "Go away!"

Ivy held up the yellow rope. It was shaking a little. Most grown-ups at least pretended to like kids. Not Mrs. Trantz. "We were wondering—"

"Speak up!"

"We were wondering," Ivy said a little louder.

"Stop whispering!"

Ivy's face turned red and the rope shook a little more. "We—" she began, and now her voice was shaking, too.

Most of the time, Bean was scared of Mrs. Trantz. But sometimes she couldn't stand her more than she was scared of her. This was one of those times. Bean charged through the white gravel, grabbed Ivy's arm, and hauled her toward the porch. "Look, Mrs. Trantz," she yelled. "We found this rope! Is it yours?" She waved the rope at Mrs. Trantz.

"I don't know what you're talking about!" yelled Mrs. Trantz. "I don't have rope! Go home!"

Bean knew how to drive Mrs. Trantz around the bend. She stepped right up beside her and smiled with all her teeth. "Great! Thanks, Mrs. Trantz!" Mrs. Trantz took a step back,

and Bean followed, still smiling. She put up her arms like she was about to give her a big hug. Mrs. Trantz squeaked and scuttled back inside her house.

"Go!" she shouted. "Go along!" She waved her hands to dust them away.

+ + + + + +

Back in the P. I. office, they agreed that no one had lied. No one looked to one side, covered their mouths, or pulled their ears. Eleanor-who-lived-in-the-blue-house hadn't really answered, but she hadn't acted like she owned the rope, either. They decided that the rope didn't belong to anyone on Pancake Court. There were no suspects.

Bean rubbed her face.

Dino and Ruby and Trevor and Prairie and Sophie S. watched her in a worried way. "So what are you going to do next?" asked Sophie S.

Bean leaned back in her chair. Whoops! That was the broken part. She sat up. "I'm going to do some hard thinking," she said. Al Seven had said the same thing when he was sitting in his car.

"Thinking about *what?*" asked Prairie.

"Secret," said Bean. She straightened her papers. "Tomorrow morning, I will reveal my plan."

They all nodded in a worried way, and then they went home, very quietly, except Ivy.

Bean spun in her chair. She slammed her phone down a few times.

"Do you have a plan?" asked Ivy.

"Sure!" said Bean. She spun around a few more times. They believed her. She was the P. I. of Pancake Court, just like she had wanted to be. Dino and Sophie S. and Ruby and Trevor and Prairie were all expecting her to catch Mr. Whoever-tied-the-yellow-rope. They were going to be mad if she didn't. "I sort of have a plan," she said. "A little bit."

Ivy twiddled her hair. "What would Al Seven do?"

"He'd sit in his car."

"You think your dad would let you sit in his car?" Ivy asked.

Bean sighed. "Probably not." When Bean was a little kid, she had locked herself in her dad's car and honked the horn. For a long time. Ever since then, she wasn't allowed to sit in the car by herself. "I don't think it would do any good anyway," she said. "It isn't sitting in the car that solves Al's cases. It's thinking."

Ivy nodded. "Okay." She watched Bean think.

Bean thought. The more she thought, the more she didn't know who had tied the yellow rope. How did Al Seven do it?

"Maybe it'll come to you in a dream," said Ivy. "Sometimes that happens in books."

"Maybe," said Bean.

"You'd better go to bed early," said Ivy.

THE BIG NAB

The next morning, Bean began to do the regular things—yawn, splash, stumble—and then she remembered the rope. Quickly she zipped out onto her front porch to take a look.

The mysterious rope-tyer had come again! The yellow rope stretched like a bright snake beyond Ivy's stairs and up Mr. Columbi's driveway, wrapped once around his garbage can, trailed across his weed collection, and moved on to Ruby and Trevor's house, where it wound in and out of their experimental bean plants and finally came to an end at the far edge of their grass.

When she saw it, Bean's heart started to thump. It grew! It was still happening! Pancake Court was a place of mystery!

Then she remembered Dino's worried face, and Sophie S.'s and Prairie's and Trevor's and Ruby's. She thought, I'm supposed to solve this mystery.

And then: How the heck am I going to do that?

She went back inside. The rest of the regular things—cereal, banana, where's my backpack, someone took it, oh here it is—didn't seem regular.

"You look tired, sweetie," said her mom. "Did you get enough sleep?"

"Hardly any," said Bean. This wasn't exactly true, but it was nice when her mom worried about her.

"She slept, Mom. She was snoring her head off when I went to bed last night," said Nancy.

"I was up half the night," said Bean. She drooped tiredly. She was about to say that she was so tired she should stay home from school, when suddenly she got the idea she'd been waiting for: the perfect plan, like something Al Seven himself might have thought up. She smiled at Nancy.

"Stop smiling at me," said Nancy grumpily.

"Sure thing, pal."

+ + + + + +

"It's in *our* yard now," said Ruby. She was chewing on her hair.

"In our *beans*," added Trevor.

"It's wrapped around Mr. Columbi's garbage can," said Dino. He looked over his shoulder and whispered, "You think it could be a zombie?"

"Or a werewolf?" said Sophie S.

They all looked at Bean with worried faces. She smiled toughly. "Don't be stooges," she said. "Zombies don't carry ropes. And werewolves can't tie knots. They have paws." She tried to talk without moving her lips. "And you should stop worrying about it, because I've got a plan. A good plan. Maybe even a great plan."

"What?" said Dino.

"She said she has a plan," Ivy explained. "A good plan, maybe even a great plan."

"Tell it," said Ruby. Trevor and Prairie and Sophie S. nodded.

Bean looked around at their scared faces. It was her job to make them feel better. "Okay. Here's my plan. Mr. Whoever-tied-the-rope comes in the night, right?" They nodded. "So tonight, I'm going to get up in the middle of the night and wait for him. When he comes out to tie the rope, I'll nab him!"

"What does that mean, *nab*?" asked Trevor.

"Um, get him," Bean said. "Grab him."

"What if he's big and mean?" asked Sophie worriedly.

Yikes, Bean thought. What if he *is* big and mean?

"I know," said Ivy. "Just take a picture of him. That way you don't have to get close to him. You can take a picture and then run back inside and lock the door."

"Good idea," said Bean. "I'll take a picture of him."

"I'd do it with you, except my mom would freak," said Trevor.

"Ha," said Ruby. "*You'd* freak."

"I would not!"

"Who has three night-lights?" said Ruby.

"I don't have three!" yelled Trevor. "I do not!"

After they yelled at each other for a while, Bean interrupted. "It's okay, I'll do it myself. Danger makes me laugh."

She hoped it would, anyway.

+ + + + + +

"Guess I'll go to bed now!" said Bean.

"What?" Her mom looked up from her book. "It's only eight."

"Remember? I hardly slept last night." Bean tried to droop.

"Oh, right," said her mom. "You want me to come up and tuck you in?"

Bean opened her mouth wide. She hoped it looked like a yawn. "That's okay. I don't want to bother you."

Her mother seemed surprised. "Wow. Okay. Nighty-night."

Bean went upstairs. 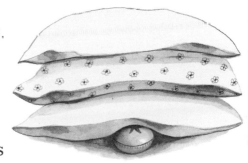 The real reason she didn't want her mother to tuck her in was under her pillow. It was a timer shaped like a tomato. Bean didn't know how to set an alarm clock, but she did know how to set a timer: You twisted it all the way around. It would tick off an hour, and then a really loud bell would ring. That's why it was under Bean's pillow. Actually, it was under Bean's pillow plus two other pillows. Bean could still hear it from under three pillows, but she didn't think her parents would.

Bean turned out her light and jumped into bed. She needed to go to sleep right away,

because she only had an hour before the timer would ring. Then she would twist it again, for another hour. She would twist it four times, and then it would be midnight, and she would get up and go outside.

Bean kicked her sheets, thinking about big and mean rope-tying people, about the timer waking her parents up, about sitting on her porch in the dark. She thought so much that when the timer rang, she had only been asleep for a few minutes. She twisted it again, and went back to sleep.

She twisted it again, and went back to sleep.

She twisted it again, and went back to sleep.

DANGER MAKES
THEM YAWN

She twisted it again—No! Midnight! Time to get up!

Very quietly, Bean put on her clothes. She stood still and listened to make sure no one was awake. The only sound was her own breathing. Danger makes me laugh, she reminded herself. But she was too tired to laugh, and anyway, if she laughed, her mom might wake up. Bean slipped out of her room and went downstairs. She stopped in her mom's office to borrow her phone, the one with the camera, and then she got the flashlight, and finally there was nothing else to do except go outside.

In the front hallway, Bean took a deep breath. She got ready for the dark and the cold and maybe a big and mean person. Everyone else was cozy in their warm beds. Nobody knew what she was doing. She was all alone. Al Seven never seemed lonely. There was something weird about him, Bean decided. She opened the door.

The porch looked regular, but the rest of Pancake Court was blueish-blackish and empty. Bean sat down on her top step, and looked out over the nighttime world, with its loom- ing, dark houses and rustling, dark trees. The yellow rope glowed in the light of the streetlamp, from Dino's chimney to Ruby and Trevor's grass. She had made it in time. It hadn't grown, not yet. The nighttime world reminded her of Al Seven's black-and-white world. Even though she wasn't cold, Bean shivered. It wasn't the rope. It was the alone.

Click. As Bean watched, Ivy came quietly out her front door. She looked over at Bean's house and waved. Then she ran down her front stairs to the sidewalk and around Pancake Court, all the way to Bean's house.

To heck with Al Seven, Bean thought as she watched Ivy run. To heck with laughing at danger. To heck with being tough. Ivy was the greatest. "Hi!" she whispered, as Ivy came up the driveway. "How'd you get up?"

"Timer," whispered Ivy, sitting down beside Bean.

"Me too! Is yours a tomato?"

"Nope, an egg," said Ivy. She lookcd at the rope. "It hasn't gotten longer."

Bean scooted close to her. "I'm glad you came."

"I want to see Mr. Whoever-tied-the-rope," said Ivy.

"You do? What if he's big and mean?" asked Bean.

"Maybe he'll be little and nice."

Bean hoped so.

They did some waiting. They did some more

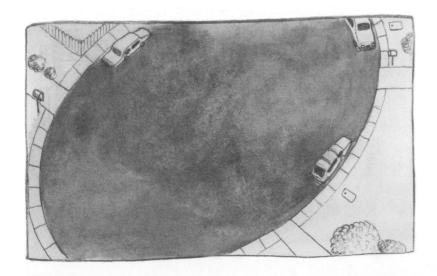

waiting. They did some huddling. Then some more waiting. Then their tushes fell asleep. They got to their feet and did some stand up waiting. They sat down and waited some more.

Nothing happened.

Bean put her head down on her knees for a while. The while stretched on. She might have closed her eyes.

She opened them and looked across the street. The rope had grown again. Bright and yellow, it crossed the street and went under

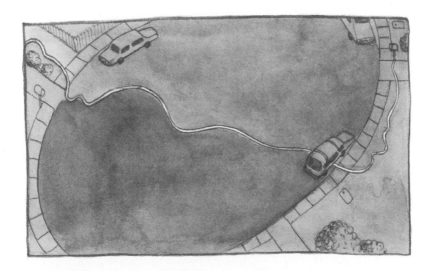

Jake the Teenager's car, which was parked at the curb. Then it went up Jake the Teenager's lawn and over his driveway and up to Kalia's mailbox.

Bean nudged Ivy. "Wake up. It happened."

"I'm awake," said Ivy, even though she wasn't. She opened her eyes. "Wow," she said after a minute. "He must be pretty quiet, Mr. Whoever."

"Yeah," said Bean. Mr. Whoever was quiet. He wasn't big and mean. That was an idea that came from being scared. And being scared came from not understanding why anyone would stretch rope all over Pancake Court. Bean didn't understand why either, but she was sure, now, that it wasn't a mean person who had done it. Suddenly, she thought maybe it wasn't even a person. Maybe it was a creature from another world. She pictured a

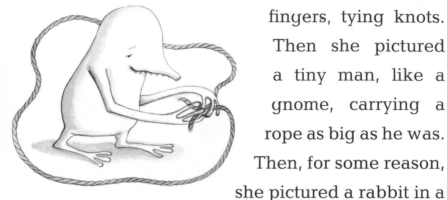

soft thing with long, white, rubbery fingers, tying knots. Then she pictured a tiny man, like a gnome, carrying a rope as big as he was. Then, for some reason, she pictured a rabbit in a cowboy hat with a yellow rope lasso. "It could be anything tying that rope," she said.

Ivy nodded happily. "I know! Isn't it great? It could be an invisible being."

"It could be a creature from another world," Bean said. "With long, white, rubbery fingers."

"Yeah!" said Ivy. Her face got dreamy. "Or maybe the rope *is* the creature. Maybe it's tying itself." She looked at Bean. "Like magic."

Bean nodded. "Maybe it's magic." She leaned forward to look at the rope. It was either a mystery or magic. Either way was fine. "It's going to get to my house soon."

"You'll have a mystery in your own front yard," said Ivy.

A mystery in her own front yard. Right in the middle of her P. I. office. "Al Seven is always wanting to solve mysteries," Bean said.

"That's what I don't get about him," said Ivy. "Why does he always want to *solve* them?

You solve problems, but a mystery isn't a problem, so why does it have to be solved?"

"Sometimes it's a problem," said Bean.

"This one isn't. Nobody's getting hurt or anything. It's a nice mystery."

Bean nodded. It was true. The rope moved from yard to yard. It wasn't doing anything bad. It came in the night and no one knew who did it, but that made it interesting.

Ivy yawned.

Yawns were catching. Bean yawned, too.

Ivy stood up. "I'm going home."

"Okay. See you tomorrow." Bean watched until Ivy closed her door, and then she went upstairs to her own cozy bed.

AT THE END OF THEIR ROPE

"You didn't get him!" yelled Trevor when Bean came out of her house the next morning.

"You fell asleep, didn't you?" said Ruby.

"Did you even get up at all?" asked Dino.

They crowded together, waiting for her on the sidewalk.

"I *was* up," Bean said. "Ivy and I were both up all night, sitting right on the porch there. In the dark. Without a single light," she added to Trevor.

"Well?" said Prairie. She pointed to the rope on Kalia's mailbox.

"Well, okay, we didn't see who did it," Bean admitted. "It was very strange and mysterious. One moment it wasn't there, and the next moment it was. We're thinking that maybe it's some kind of white, rubbery creature from another world who comes every night with a piece of rope."

"And slithers through the bushes without making any sound," Ivy added, coming up to the group. "And then—"

"Cut it out, you guys!" said Sophie S.

"Yeah, cut it out!" said Dino. He looked mad.

"But it's cool!" Bean said. She tried to explain. "It could be a regular person, but he'd have to be tiny, like a gnome or—"

"A gnome?" asked Dino. "Like a little creepy guy? That's not cool!"

Sophie S. put her hands on her hips. "Listen, Bean, you said you would catch

Mr. Whoever. You *said.*"

"Yeah," said Trevor and Ruby and Prairie together.

Bean tried again. "But it could be magic! Right here in our own neighborhood! Isn't that the greatest?"

"Zombies are magic," said Dino. "And then they eat your brains."

"I think you guys watch too many scary movies," said Bean. "This is real life. It's our very own mystery, and, it might even be magic."

There was a silence. Then Trevor said, "If we knew for sure it was magic, it would be okay."

"But we don't know what it is," said Ruby.

"And we don't know why it's happening," said Sophie.

"Right!" said Ivy, waving her hands in the air. "That's what makes it a mystery!"

She and Bean smiled at the faces around them. Nobody smiled back.

"Okay, Bean," said Prairie after a moment. "If you won't solve the Mystery of the Yellow Rope, then we will."

Sheesh. They were so serious. "Fine!" said Bean. "I'll solve it, I'll solve it! Meet me in the P. I. office after school."

All day, Bean thought about magic and Al Seven and being a P. I. But most of all, she thought about solving the Mystery of the

Yellow Rope. She thought about it during rug time. She thought about it during Drop Everything and Read. She thought about it during Mad Minute Math. She even thought about it during recess.

By the end of the day, she still hadn't solved a thing. The case was uncracked.

After school, Ivy and Bean walked home. They walked very slowly. Then they walked backward. Then they played Straightjacket, where you could only turn when you ran into something. It took a long time to get back to Pancake Court. The closer they got, the slower they walked.

"What am I going to do?" asked Bean. "I'm supposed to solve the mystery."

"Maybe you could say that a zombie *did* eat your brains," Ivy suggested. "Nobody can solve a mystery if her brain has been eaten."

Dino and Ruby and Trevor and Sophie S. and Prairie were already sitting in the P. I. office on the lawn.

"We've made a decision," Trevor said as soon as he saw Bean.

"Great!" said Bean. Making all the decisions was wearing her out.

"Our decision is that we should tell the grown-ups," said Prairie. "They'll never notice on their own."

"Tell them what?" asked Ivy.

"That some creepy person is tying up Pancake Court!" squeaked Trevor.

What? "That's not what's happening!" said Bean.

"That's a terrible decision!" said Ivy at the same time.

"We have to tell a grown-up," said Sophie.

"No! They'll get all upset," said Bean.

She looked over at the bright yellow rope, almost at her yard. "They'll untie the rope and throw it away."

"They'll catch whoever it is!" said Dino.

"Yeah, and if it's all slithery and white like you said, they'll—" Trevor made a blowing-up sound.

Ivy and Bean looked at each other with wide eyes. Blowing up magical creatures from other worlds? That was horrible. "You'll hurt it!" Ivy cried.

"You said you were going to solve the mystery, Bean," said Sophie S. "But you didn't. There's nothing else to do but tell a grown-up."

CRACK!

Bean rubbed her face, for real this time. There had to be a way to keep them from telling a grown-up about the rope, and she needed to think of it in the next three seconds.

Ivy sniffed.

Bean wondered what would happen if she tied herself up in the rope. They wouldn't blow it up if she were inside it. Or would they?

Ivy sniffed louder.

Bean gave her the bug-eyed look. What?

Ivy tapped herself with one finger.

Bean pointed at Ivy. You?

Ivy nodded.

Bean lifted her eyebrows. Really?

Ivy nodded again. Go ahead.

Ivy was the most amazing person in the world. Bean smiled. Okay. She tried to remember exactly what Al Seven had said. "The end isn't always pretty," she began.

Everyone looked confused. "What?" said Ruby.

Bean sighed. She shook her head. "Friends. They break your heart, I guess."

"Whose heart?" said Sophie S. "What are you talking about?"

Bean grabbed Ivy's arm and said loudly, "Crime doesn't pay, pal!"

Ivy fell to her knees. "You got me!" she wailed, covering her face with her hands. "It was me! I did it!"

"Did what?" yelled Dino.

Ivy looked between her fingers. "I am Mr. Whoever! I tied the rope!"

"You are?" said Sophie S. and Prairie and Ruby and Trevor together. "You did?"

Ivy nodded and covered her face again, "I did it. I'm sorry!"

"No way," said Dino.

"Yes way," sniffed Ivy.

"How'd you get up on my roof?" Dino asked, looking at her with narrow eyes.

"Um—I—uh—"

Bean could tell Ivy was going to say something about flying, so quickly she interrupted, "Ivy has a super-long ladder at her house." This was true, too.

"I do!" said Ivy. "The painter left it by mistake. It's in the backyard."

"Didn't you say she was on the porch with you last night?" asked Ruby. "How could she add a new piece of rope when you were sitting right there?"

"When she fell asleep, I snuck off the porch and tied a new piece onto the end. I lied! I lied to my friend!" Ivy buried her face in her hands again.

Bean said sternly, "I hope you've learned something from this, young lady." Her parents said that to her all the time.

"I sure did," Ivy said. She lifted her face and looked into the distance in a learning sort of way. "I'll never do it again."

"Okay," said Bean. "I guess that's that." She looked at Trevor and Ruby and Prairie and Sophie S. and Dino. "So we're done!" she said loudly. "The end! Case cracked! Mystery solved!"

There was a pause. Then Dino said, "But *why*? Why did you do it?"

"To scare you," said Ivy. "To terrify you. Sorry."

There was another pause.

"I wasn't scared," said Ruby.

"Me neither," said Dino and Sophie S. together. They made snorty sounds.

"Like I'd be scared of a yellow rope!" said Prairie.

"Yeah, it was dumb," said Trevor. He got up. "I'm going. I've got stuff to do."

"Me too."

"Yeah."

"Rope! Ha! Who's scared of a rope?"

One by one, they walked away.

Ivy and Bean watched them go.

When they were finally alone, they looked at each other. "That was good," said Bean. "That was really good."

Ivy nodded. "We saved a magical creature from doom. We are friends of magic," she called loudly, just in case the magical creature was listening.

Bean leaned over her desk to take another peek at the yellow rope. "You know what? I think I'd better take this desk and stuff down. I don't want the rope to feel crowded."

"Right," said Ivy. "That was a close one."

"Yeah," said Bean. "I don't want to be a P. I. anymore. I think I'll go back to being the person who makes up fortunes for fortune cookies."

"That's a good job," said Ivy. "I'm still going to be a witch."

"I'll write a fortune that says You will soon meet a witch, and then you can come out from under the table, and the fortune will be true," said Boan. "And then everyone will want my fortunes."

Ivy nodded. "We'll be a team."

It was nice to have the future all worked out.

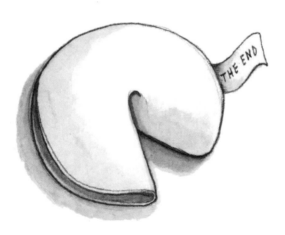

HI KIDS!

Oh boy! We are going to solve mysteries! We are going to be tough! We are going to uncover secrets! We are going to sneak and spy and follow the clues! We are going to nab the suspects, discover the answers, and know too much! We are going to have a blast! Why? Because we are private investigators, that's why!

PRIVATE EYES

Now, everyone knows that private investigators wear hats. Or sunglasses. Or both at once. Partly, they do this to look tough and cool, but the real reason is to hide their eyes. They don't want other people to know where they're looking. If you're spying on Sammy La Barba, you don't want him to know it. So you pull your hat low or you put on sunglasses, and Sammy La Barba doesn't have a clue.

But what if you don't have a hat or a pair of sunglasses? Easy-peasy! Learn how to walk with a book in front of your face. You can spy over the top of it, and other people will think you're reading! Also, grown-ups love to see kids reading, so they'll be happy.

Here's what to do: Get a not-too-heavy book and hold it up in front of your face. Keep the top edge of the book just below your eyes. Start walking, very slowly (or you'll smack into something). Look over the top of the book most of the time (or you'll smack into something) but every three steps, glance down at the book super quick, so you'll look like you're reading. The more you practice, the easier it gets. So start practicing!

SNOOPER

All private investigators have to learn how to snoop. Snooping is the same thing as noticing, especially noticing things that other people don't want you to notice. To get good at snooping, you need to train yourself to look and remember. So here's a fun game that gives you practice at looking and remembering.

Here's what to do: Set out at least twenty little things on a tray or table. Nothing fancy, just stuff like nickels and raisins and combs. Also get out a towel and a clock and a piece of paper and a pencil. Look at the little things for 30 seconds (half a minute), and then cover them up with the towel. Now, write down as many as you can remember. Did you get them all? Wow, you're practically a spy already.

You can add more things or you can shorten the time to 20 seconds if you want to make it harder. You can also take turns with another person if you like that kind of thing.

NOT TOO DUSTY

Did you know that everyone in the entire world has different fingerprints? It's true. Private investigators often nab their suspects by dusting for fingerprints. What they really do is powder for fingerprints, but they call it dusting for some reason. It's pretty fun, and you can do it, too.

Here's what to do: For once in your life, you don't need to wash your hands before you begin. It's better if your hands are kind of dirty and sticky (not wet, though). Get some baby powder and a soft paintbrush. Then get something smooth and dark, like a dark plate or mug or plastic bottle, and press your thumb hard into it. Sprinkle a little powder over the place where you pressed your thumb and then brush the powder off with the soft brush.

Oh my gosh! Do you see the thumbprint? You've found your suspect!

Oh. Wait. It's only you. But still, it was fun.

DO-IT-YOURSELF MYSTERY

Here's a secret: Grown-ups have pretty boring lives. They get up, go to work, eat dinner, and fall asleep, day after day. No wonder they think sleeping is fun. But you can help them by making their lives more interesting. You can make a mystery for your grown-up.

Here's what to do: Your mystery can be super-easy or super-complicated or somewhere in the middle. You don't want to scare your grown-up, you just want to make them wonder. For example, moving something in your house is an easy way to make a mystery. Take something that's right out where everyone can see it (but not something that your grown-up is touchy about): a picture, a vase, a book, a coffee mug. Now, move it.

Turn it around or put it somewhere else. Grown-ups don't pay a whole lot of attention to what's going on, so you might have to be patient, but eventually, they'll notice. And then, they'll wonder.

You can make a more complicated mystery by putting odd things together. Like, for example, putting a fork in the mailbox. Or blowing up a balloon and putting it in your grown-up's car. Or you can make a super-complicated mystery by leaving notes in odd places. For instance, you can write "Must see Fred about" on a piece of paper and leave it in the refrigerator. Then write "the can, and Mabel wants to know" on another piece of paper and put it under the soap. Then write "if the secret is" and drop it in the middle of the floor. It'll drive them bonkers. What a laugh!

If you do all these fun things, you'll practically be a private investigator, just like Bean, P. I., and her assistant, Ivy.

Congratulations—and don't be a stooge!

IVY + BEAN + YOU!

Personalize your own Ivy + Bean notebooks, folders and more at MyChronicleBooks.com!

Ellie's Math Homework

Kayla's Reading L

Lily's Journal

Zoey

Sophie
Sophie
Sophie

25% OFF*

*SAVE 25% off personalized school supplies.
Use code: **MYCB-IVYBEAN** at checkout.

my chronicle books
PERSONALIZED BOOKS AND GIFTS

FOLLOW IVY + BEAN ON
ALL OF THEIR ADVENTURES!

Collect them all. How many have you read?

HAVE EVEN MORE FUN WITH IVY + BEAN!

Make your own buttons!

Create your own Ivy + Bean adventures with paper dolls!

More than 90 removable stickers!

Send secret notes to your friends!

Includes fold-and-seal notes and stickers!